The Princess and the Frog

First published in 2003 by
Franklin Watts
338 Euston Road
London
NW1 3BH

Franklin Watts Australia
Level 17 / 207 Kent Street
Sydney
NSW 2000

A CIP catalogue record for this book is available
from the British Library.

ISBN 978 0 7496 5129 9

Series Editor: Jackie Hamley
Series Advisor: Dr Barrie Wade
Cover Design: Jason Anscomb
Design: Peter Scoulding

Printed in China

Franklin Watts is a division of
Hachette Children's Books,
an Hachette Livre UK company.

The
Princess
and the Frog

by Margaret Nash and Martin Remphry

W
FRANKLIN WATTS
LONDON•SYDNEY

Once upon a time, there was
a princess who didn't behave
like a princess.

She didn't sit on velvet cushions.

She wouldn't wear her crown.

The king didn't know what to
do with her.

"You are always jumping about," he said. "No prince will want to marry you!"

"I don't want to marry a boring old prince," said the princess.

The princess threw her golden ball. "OUT!" shouted the king, pointing at the door.

The princess took her ball to the far
end of the garden, and bounced it
up and down. Suddenly, the ball
went too far. It landed in the pond.

"OH NO!" cried the princess.
She lay down at the edge of the
pond and tried to reach the ball.

"Come here, ball!" she yelled, but the ball was sinking. She thought she would never see it again.

"If I get your ball, will you play with me?" The princess looked up and saw a frog sitting on a lily pad.

"Certainly," said the princess.
The frog hopped off the lily
pad and swam away.

15

The frog soon came back with
the ball in his mouth.
"Thank you," said
the princess and
she bowed
to him.

They played hopscotch on the path. "This is fun," said the princess, "but now I've got to go back to the palace for tea."

"Please let me come," said the frog.
The princess bent down. "OK," she
agreed, "hop on my shoulder."

When the king opened the door,
he threw his hands up in horror.
"Look at your dirty dress!" he said.

"And WHO is that?" he asked,

pointing at her shoulder.

"CROAK!" croaked the frog.

"He's staying for tea," said the
princess. "He found my ball and
I promised to play with him."

"Hmmm..." said the king. "Well, a promise is a promise, I suppose."

The frog jumped onto the table and the princess fed him some cake. "His table manners are terrible!" said the king.

After tea, the frog asked: "May I
sleep in your room, princess?"
"Tell him no!" said the king.

But the princess picked up the frog
and carried him to her bedroom.

She put him in the sink. She loved
his big goggle eyes and wide smile.

"Let's stay friends," she said, and
she kissed his silky green nose.

"Forever?" he croaked.

"Yes, forever!" she croaked back.
And they hopped out of the
palace and down to the
pond where they lived
happily ever after.